FALL IS HERE!
I LOVE IT!

by Elaine W. Good
Illustrated by Susie Shenk Wenger

Good 🌳 Books®

Intercourse, PA17534
800/762-7171
www.goodbks.com

International Standard Book Number: 1-56148-142-4
Library of Congress Catalog Card Number: 90-71115

Library of Congress Cataloging-in-Publication Data

Good, Elaine W., 1944-
   Fall is here! I love it! / Elaine W. Good; illustrated
by Susie Shenk Wenger.
   p. cm.
   Summary: A young child enjoys the sights, colors,
tastes, and smells as fall comes to the family farm.
[1. Autumn—Fiction. 2. Farm life—Fiction.] I.
Wenger, Susie Shenk, 1956- ill. II. Title.
PZ7.G5996Fal 1990   90-71115
[E]—dc20]   CIP
                                                AC

Everything is coming down! Leaves are falling. Nuts are dropping. Ripe apples and pears plunk on the ground. In the garden, flower seed heads droop low. Today some neighbors are coming to help Daddy cut down the field corn and blow it into the silo.

Fall is here! I love it!

School started last week. David, Caroline and Christine ride away in the school bus every morning. I am the only one left to help Daddy clean up the barn. I can sweep troughs all by myself.

Fall is here! I love it!

Some days the air is chilly and I want to wear a jacket. But when Mommy and I take a hike to pick the last tea in the meadow, our sweaters are too warm, so we take them off. Along the fences pokeberries are growing. We squash some, watching their dark purple juice stain our fingers.

Fall is here! I love it!

The cows are in the meadow too, enjoying the warm sunshine. They graze quietly, eating only the grass. The beautiful ironweed growing all around them must be bitter because they don't even bite it off.

Fall is here! I love it!

For me the best part of fall is picking corn. Daddy's tractor pulls the corn picker through the fields. It gobbles up the corn stalks and spits the ears into a wagon. When the wagon is full, Mommy and I unload it. I slide down the heaps of bright yellow corn, kicking and shoving it until the wagon is empty.

Fall is here! I love it!

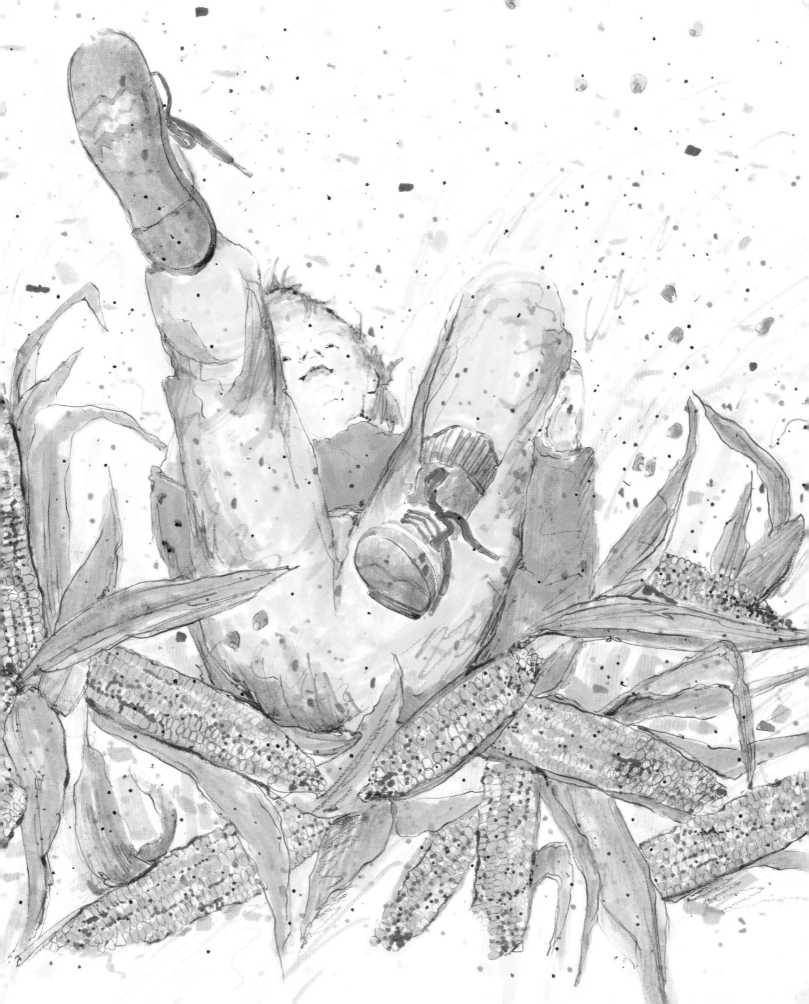

The trees are changing to new colors! In our yard and in the meadow we see yellow, brown and red ones. The leaves dance in the wind, spinning on their toes as they fall to the ground. We rake them up and heap them in the cart. I jump on them to pack them down. "Cover me up!" I shout.

Fall is here! I love it!

Goats are funny creatures! They look so smart! We watch our friend Mary milk her goats. One of them nibbles on my shoulder, tickling me and making me laugh.

Fall is here! I love it!

Mommy wants pretty flowers next spring. We must plant bulbs now, so I help
to dig and put the crinkly brown things in the ground.

Fall is here! I love it!

tulip

hyacinth

Row after row of corn is still being picked. The wagons go back and forth to the fields and we count, 1, 2, 3, 4, 5, 6, 7, 8, 9, . . . 10 loads in the corn barn today! As we walk to the house in the darkness, we hear a pheasant crowing. He sounds so proud. I hope we get to see him sometime!

Fall is here! I love it!

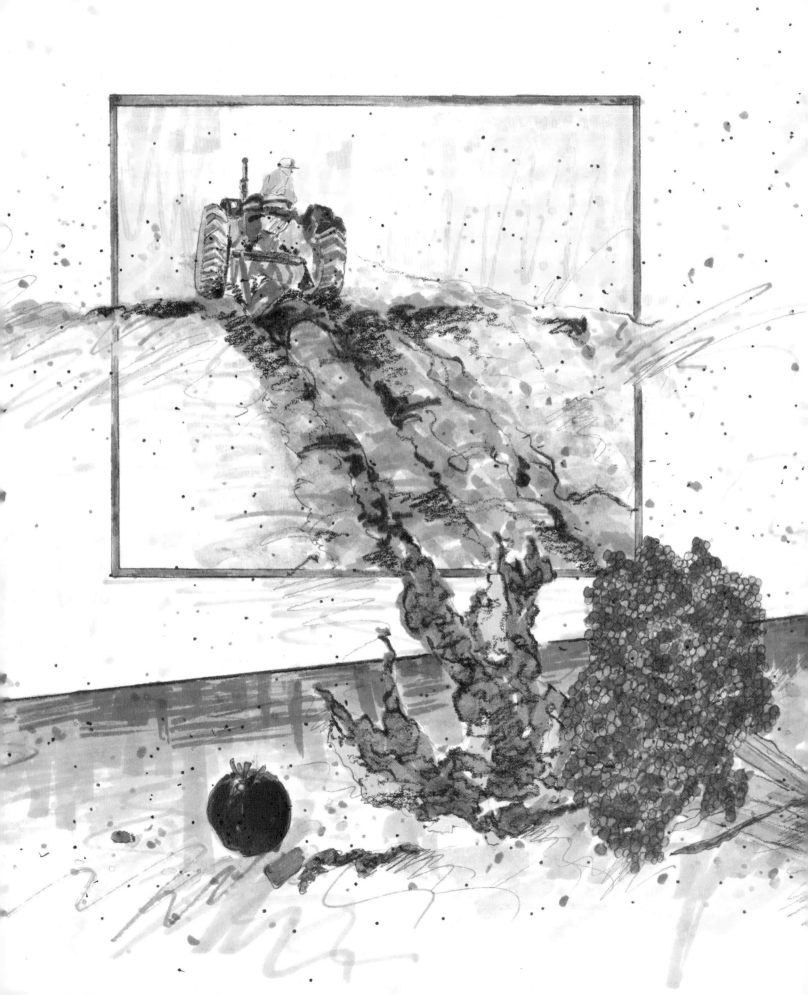

The garden needs to be put to sleep, Mommy says. We pick the last spinach, cauliflower and broccoli and carry away the stalks. And then magic! Daddy plows the garden, turning the ground over until it is all one color. I try to run after the plow but the ground is bumpy and I fall down in the soft dirt.

Fall is here! I love it!

"Apple cider! Apple cider! Bound to make your belly wider," chants Mommy as I sip a big cup full of the delicious stuff. Apples from our tree were dumped into the cider press and squeezed to make gallons of cider.

Fall is here! I love it!

Our neighbor Jake has pigs on his farm. They snort and snuffle as they roll around in the puddle at the corner of their lot. Mommy says they need the mud because they can't sweat. I wonder if they need mud on chilly days too.

Fall is here! I love it!

Guess what! This morning a pheasant strutted across the lane. When he
spied me he crouched low and darted into the corn stubble.

Fall is here! I love it!

Pumpkins! Pumpkins! Pumpkins! We discovered lots of them in the corn fields. I can just taste the good pies Mommy will bake.

Fall is here! I love it!

I help to carry Mommy's pies into Grandma's house for Thanksgiving dinner. In the pantry Grandma winks at me and slips a piece of pink candy into my hand. "To eat after dinner," she smiles.

Snowflakes hit my nose as we leave to go home. "Is it winter now?" I ask. "Almost," Mommy replies. In the car I dream of falling things: leaves, nuts, apples and snowflakes.

Winter is coming!

Elaine W. Good lives on a farm near Lititz, Pa. She and her husband are parents to two sons and two daughters.

Susie Shenk Wenger is an illustrator who lives in State College, Pa., with her husband and young daughter.

That's What Happens When It's Spring!, *It's Summertime!*, and *White Wonderful Winter!* are the other books in this seasonal series by Good and Shenk Wenger.